The toyshop

Story by Gill Munton
Pictures by Bill Piggins

Ben

Liz

Mum

Dad

the toysh
a
b
c
Open

1
2
3

sing song party

out now
books
Cats
Dogs
new
hello

Ships
Cats
Birds
flags
Tom
new

ches
che
cray
Paint
Poems
the toyshop

chess
chess
crayons
Paint set
1000
Stickers
fairy tales
1
2
3

jigsaw
200 Pieces
jigsaw
200 Pieces
jigsaw
200 Pieces

fairy tales